This book belongs to
my friend:

A NOTE TO PARENTS

In *Dora's Underwater Voyage,* Dora loses her special bracelet. In order to retrieve it, she must use her Spanish language skills to make her way through each step of the rescue mission. By repeating the Spanish words with Dora, your child will experience the excitement of learning a new language.

As you read through the book the first time, pay special attention to the words that appear in both English and Spanish in the illustrations. Recite both the Spanish and English words. If you are not familiar with Spanish, use the pronunciation guide at the front of the book to help you pronounce the words correctly. Continue by reading the story a second time. When you come to the words that appear in English and Spanish, read the English and pause to ask your child if he remembers the equivalent Spanish word. Also try to use some of these words daily to reinforce what your child has learned.

If you are interested in having your child learn a second language, it is a good idea to start when he is young. Studies show that learning a new language is easier for children than for adults. Many types of language programs have been developed with kids specifically in mind. As the world continues to grow smaller, knowing more than one language is an increasingly important lifelong skill.

Learning Fundamental: **reading + language**

For more parent and kid-friendly activities, go to www.nickjr.com.

Dora's Underwater Voyage

ENGLISH/SPANISH GLOSSARY and PRONUNCIATION GUIDE

English	Spanish	Pronunciation
Thank you	Gracias	GRAH-see-ahs
Hello	Hola	OH-lah
Open.	Ábrete.	AH-breh-tay
Gate	La puerta	LAH PWER-tah
Whale	La ballena	LAH bah-YEH-nah
Clam.	La almeja.	LAH ahl-MAY-hah
Window	La ventana	LAH ben-TAH-nah
Claw	La garra	LAH GAH-rrah

Published by Scholastic Inc., 90 Old Sherman Turnpike, Danbury, CT 06816

ISBN 0-7172-6653-2

Printed in the U.S.A.

First Scholastic Printing, March 2003

Dora's Underwater Voyage

by
Christine Ricci

illustrated by
Jason Fruchter

SCHOLASTIC INC.

New York Toronto London Auckland Sydney
Mexico City New Delhi Hong Kong Buenos Aires

One day, Dora and Boots were playing at the beach. Suddenly a wave splashed against Dora. Her bracelet fell off and floated away into the ocean!

"Oh no!" said Dora. "My bracelet was a present from my Mami and Papi! I have to get it back!"

"How will we find your bracelet?" asked Boots.
"The ocean is so big, and your bracelet is so small."

"Hmm," thought Dora. "Who helps us when we don't know where to go?"

"Map!" Dora and Boots called.

Map popped out of Backpack's side pocket.

"I can tell you where the bracelet is," said Map. "It's at the Sunken Ship. First you have to go through the Seaweed Gate, then past the Clams, and that's how you'll get to the Sunken Ship to find the bracelet."

"*Gracias,* Map," Dora said.

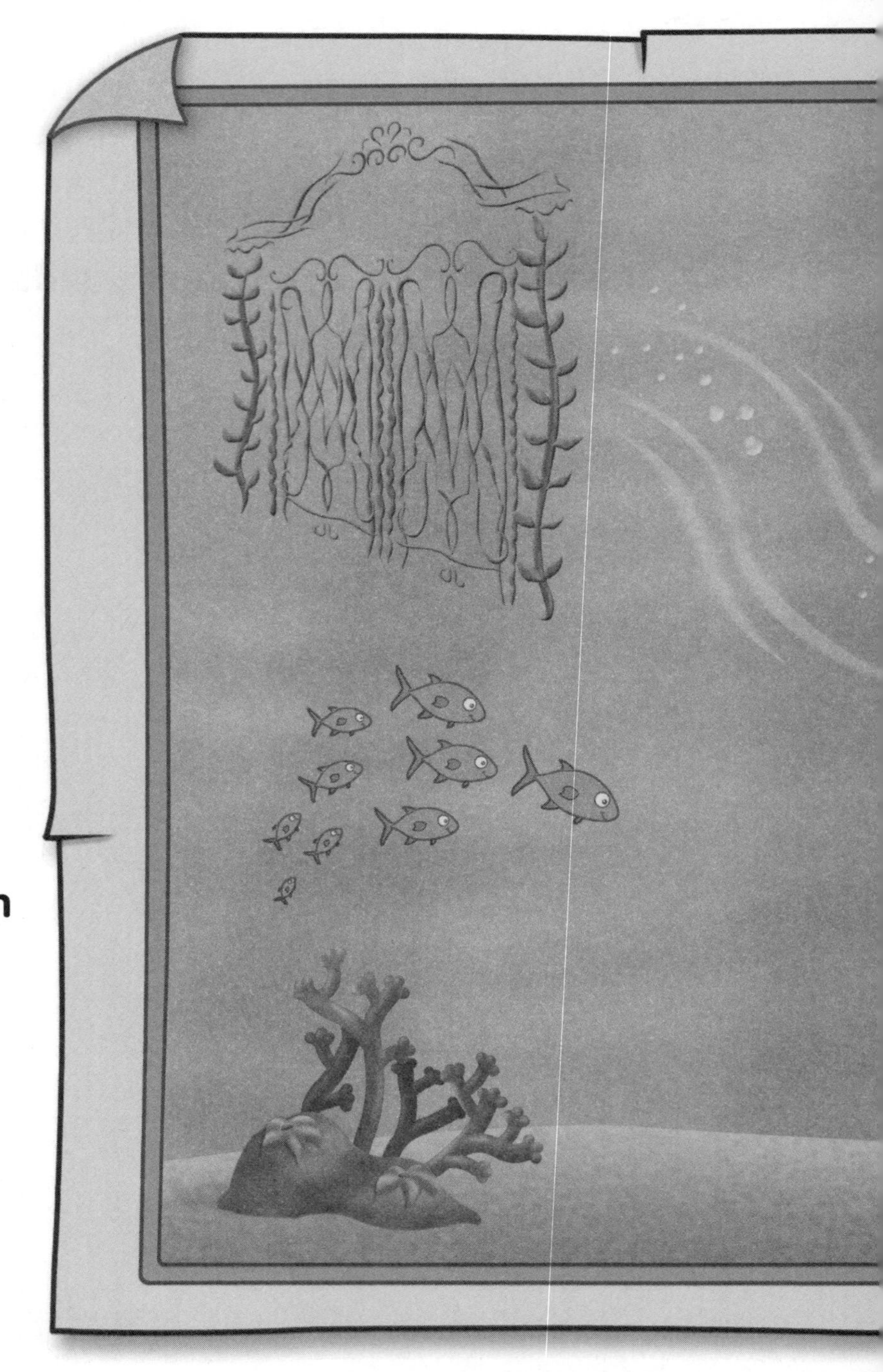

"Do you see something we can use to take us deep into the ocean?" asked Dora.

Boots looked around. "I see a submarine!" he shouted. "It can take us underwater."

“Great idea,” said Dora.

They dragged the submarine to the water, opened the hatch, and climbed inside.

As the submarine slowly traveled toward the ocean floor, a sea horse appeared.

"*¡Hola!*" said the sea horse. "Where are you going?"

"We're looking for the Sunken Ship to find my bracelet," Dora explained.

"Oh," said the sea horse. "To get there, you'll need to know the secret word, so remember this:

To open things along your way,
Just say the Spanish word *¡Ábrete!*"

Dora and Boots thanked the sea horse and continued on their way.

"There's the Seaweed Gate," Boots shouted. "But it's closed. How will we get through so we can get to the Sunken Ship?"

"I'll try doing what the sea horse told us to do," Dora said. "*¡Ábrete, puerta!*"

The Seaweed Gate opened, and they traveled through it and out the other side.

“Where do we go next?” asked Boots.

“Seaweed Gate, Clams, Sunken Ship,” said Dora. “We went through the Seaweed Gate, so the Clams are next. Do you see the Clams?”

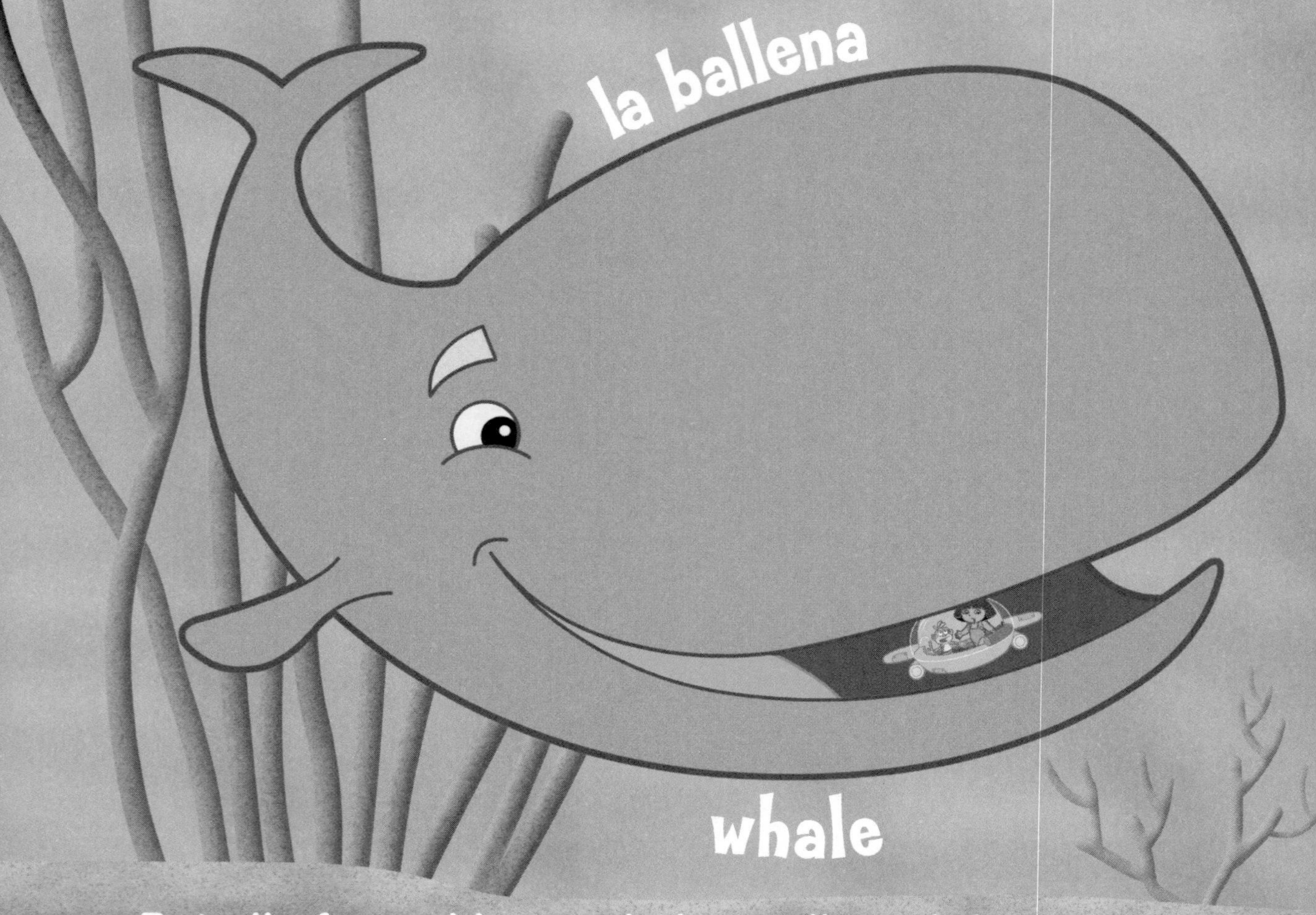

But all of a sudden a whale swallowed the submarine!

"Oh no!" cried Dora. "How will we get to the Sunken Ship to find my bracelet?"

"Open, whale!" shouted Boots. But the whale didn't open.

"Remember what the sea horse said!" said Dora.

"*¡Ábrete, ballena!*" yelled Dora and Boots.

The whale opened its mouth, and Dora and Boots quickly drove the submarine back into the sea.

Soon Dora and Boots arrived at the Clams. They steered the submarine around the first clam, over the second clam, and past the third clam. But the fourth clam snapped down on the submarine.

"We're trapped!" called Dora. "But we know what to do to get this clam to open!"

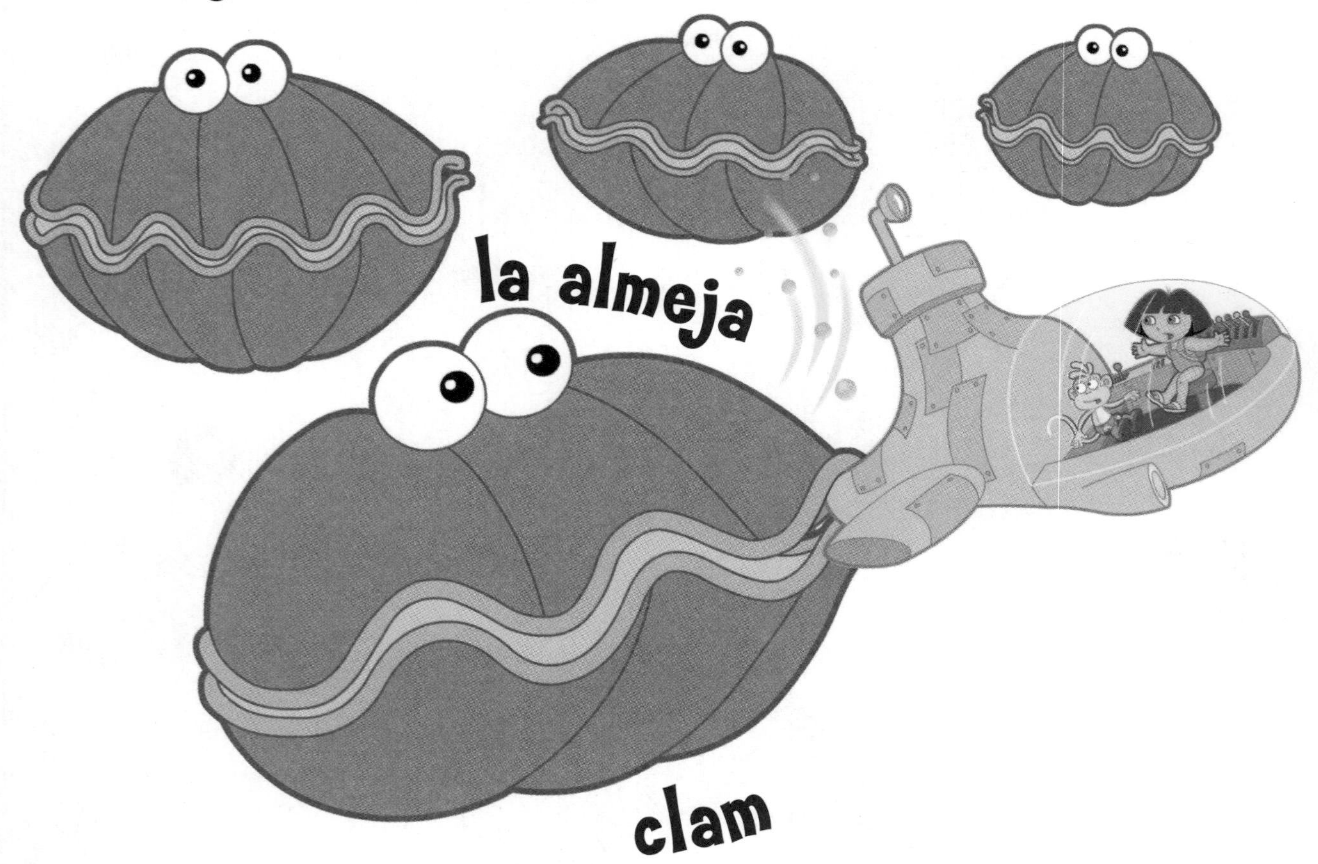

"*¡Ábrete, almeja!*" Dora and Boots called as loudly as they could.

The clam heard them and opened up to set them free.

"Whew! That was close!" said Boots. "Come on, let's go find the bracelet!"

"There's the Sunken Ship!" Boots cried. "How will we get inside?"

"We'll have to open a window," replied Dora.

la ventana

window

"*¡Ábrete, ventana!*" **Dora and Boots shouted.**

The window opened, and the submarine dived through the window and into the ship.

The ship was filled with sparkling, glimmering treasure.

"Do you see my special bracelet?" Dora asked.

Boots pointed at a barrel behind the biggest treasure chest. "There it is."

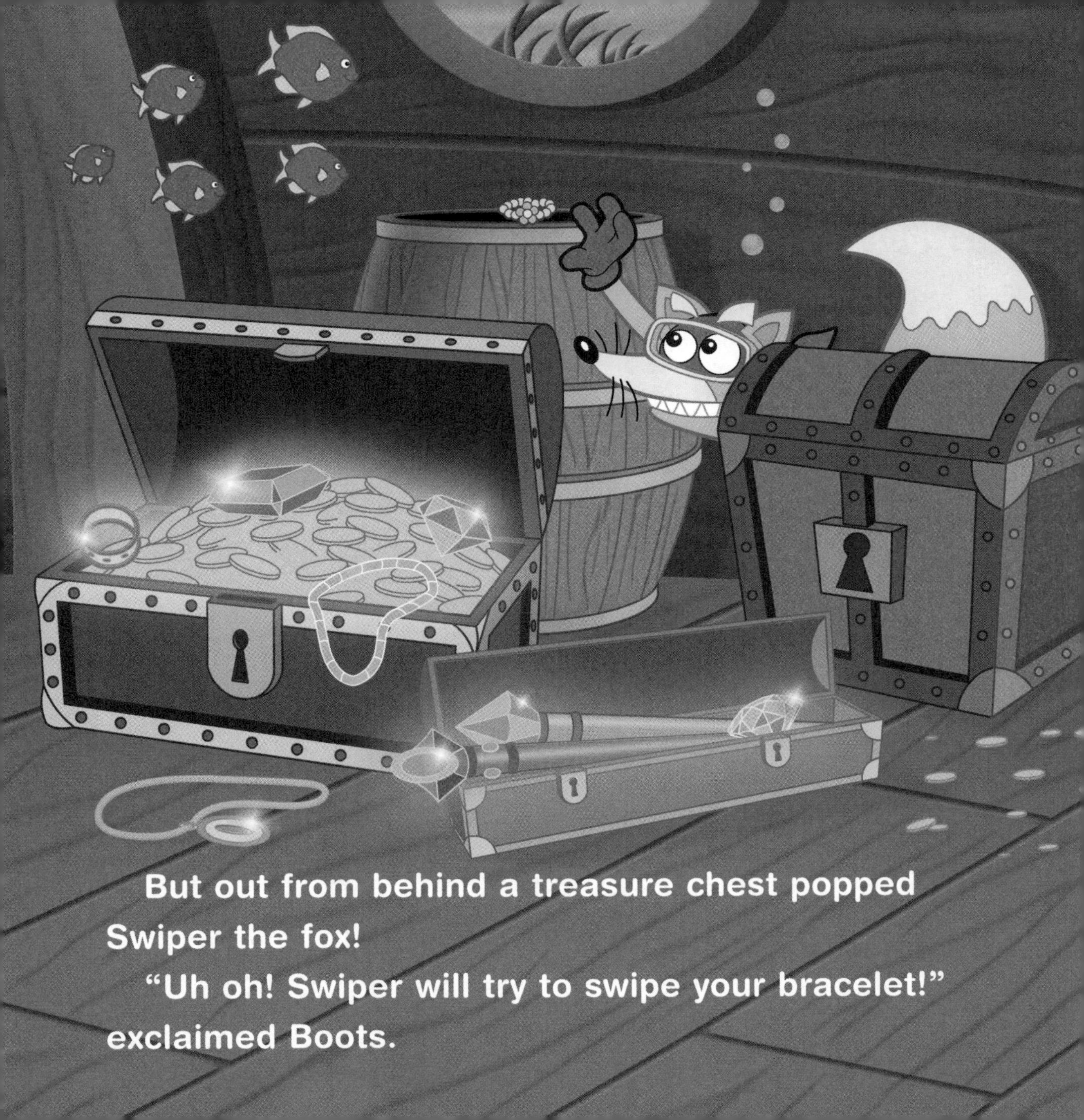

But out from behind a treasure chest popped Swiper the fox!

"Uh oh! Swiper will try to swipe your bracelet!" exclaimed Boots.

Just in time Dora and Boots yelled together, "Swiper, no swiping!"

"Oh mannn," Swiper groaned. Then he turned and swam away.

“Hooray! We stopped Swiper!”
said Boots. “Now let’s get your bracelet!”

Dora and Boots pushed some buttons in the submarine, and a giant claw popped out. The claw scooped up the bracelet and brought it over to the submarine.

"Now we have to get the claw to open so I can get my bracelet," said Dora.

"*¡Ábrete, garra!*" shouted Dora and Boots.

The claw opened and dropped the bracelet into the submarine.

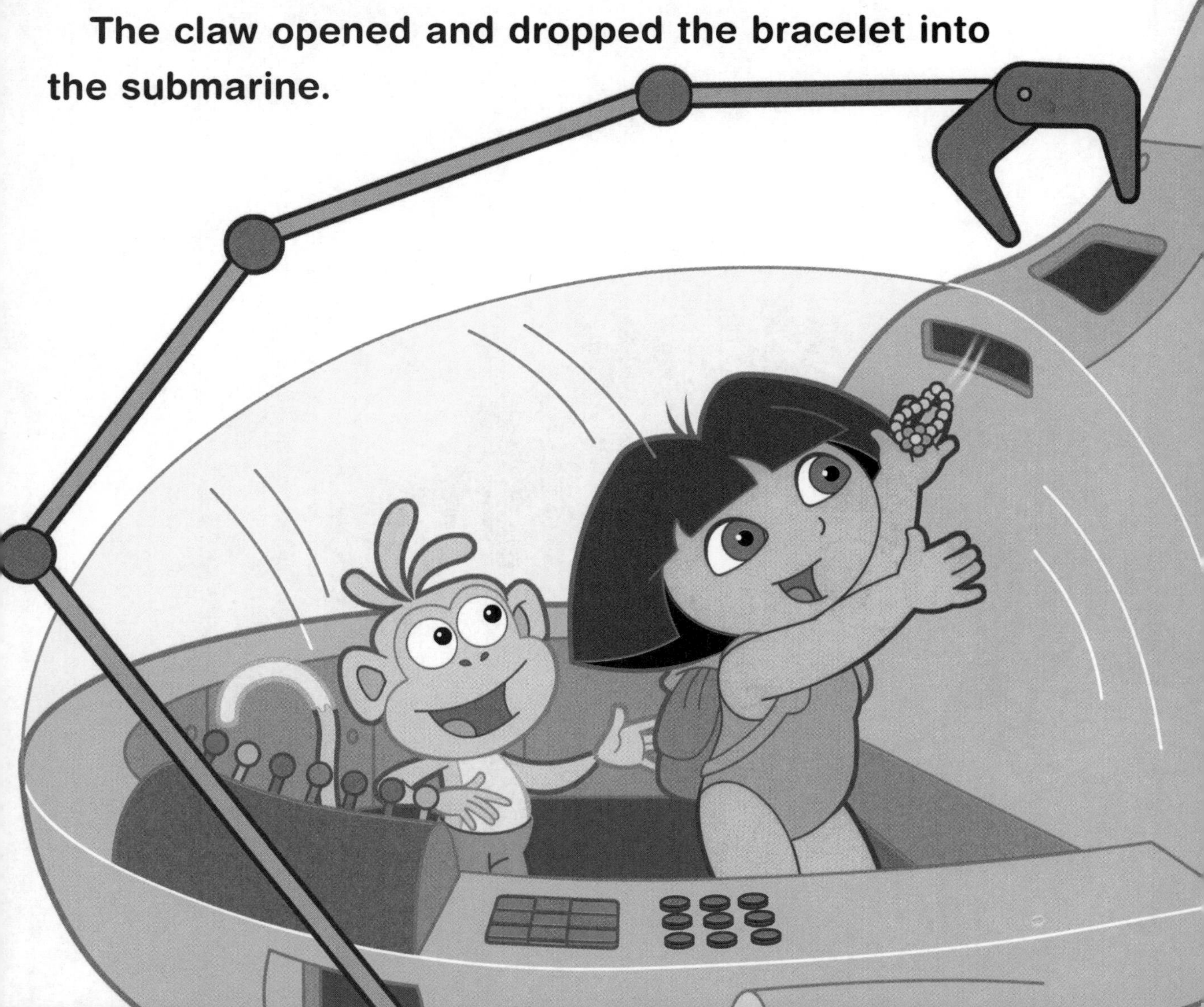

"I'm so happy to have my bracelet back!" said Dora, putting the bracelet on her wrist.

Just then the sea horse swam up next to the submarine. The sea horse said:

"Hooray! You did it! You found your way,
And rescued the bracelet by saying *¡Ábrete!*"